Care Bears™
A Very Grumpy THANKSGIVING

Written by Jenny McPherson
Illustrated by Jay Johnson

SCHOLASTIC INC.

New York Toronto London Auckland Sydney
Mexico City New Delhi Hong Kong Buenos Aires

ISBN-13: 978-0-545-07610-4

ISBN-10: 0-545-07610-2

Printed in the U.S.A.

First printing, October 2008

Designed by Michael Massen

It was Thanksgiving in Care-a-lot, and all of the Care Bears were in a good mood. Everyone, that is, except for Grumpy Bear.

"Yuck!" Crumpy Bear grumbled. "What a gray and gloomy day. I feel grumpy."
Grumpy did not remember that it was Thanksgiving.

Grumpy decided to make himself some breakfast. He poured a glass of orange juice and put two slices of bread in the toaster.

A few minutes later,
he smelled something burning.

"Oh, no!" Grumpy exclaimed. His toast was ruined. "Now I'm *super* grumpy," he said.

KNOCK, KNOCK.

What now? thought Grumpy.

There was someone at the door. It was Cheer Bear.

"I've come to wish you a happy Thanksgiving," she said.

"Thanksgiving!" Grumpy exclaimed.
"Today is the grumpiest day *ever*. What
is there to possibly be thankful for?"

"Oh, Grumpy, there are *lots* of things to be thankful for," Cheer Bear said. "Come with me and I'll show you!"

Cheer and Grumpy ran into Good Luck Bear walking down the path.

"Happy Thanksgiving!" Good Luck Bear said to his friends.

"It is *not* a happy Thanksgiving," Grumpy complained.
"There's nothing to be thankful for!"

"But look at the sky!" exclaimed Good Luck Bear.
The sun had come out, and a rainbow stretched across
Care-a-lot.

"I'm thankful for good luck," shouted Good Luck Bear.

Good Luck Bear joined Cheer and Grumpy. Then they saw Funshine Bear jumping in a pile of leaves.

"Come on!" Funshine said.

"Well . . ." said Grumpy Bear slowly, "that *does* look like it might be fun."

Soon the four friends were laughing and jumping in the leaves together.
"I am thankful for fun times with friends," Funshine said.

"I know what we should do now," suggested Good Luck Bear.
"Let's go to Share Bear's house and help her get ready for dinner."
"Great idea," Cheer Bear said. "Hooray for Thanksgiving spirit!"

Share Bear's house was bustling with activity. Everyone was preparing for Thanksgiving. Share was making dinner, and Champ Care Bear was decorating the house.

"Hi guys," Champ Care Bear said. "You're just in time to help set the table."

Grumpy Bear laid out the silverware, and Good Luck Bear, Cheer, and Funshine helped with the decorations.

Soon the table was ready.
"Thanks for your teamwork!"
Champ Care Bear said.

Finally, it was time for dinner. The Care Bears seated themselves at Share Bear's big table. Share brought out the turkey.

"I'm thankful to share this wonderful meal with all of you," she said.

"And I'm thankful that we get to eat!" exclaimed Wish Bear. "That's just what my belly was wishing for."

Everyone laughed as they filled their plates.

It was a very happy Thanksgiving feast. The Care Bears talked, laughed, and ate lots of turkey, cranberry sauce, sweet potatoes, and pumpkin pie.

"That meal was delicious, Share," said Cheer Bear. "I'm thankful to have spent Thanksgiving with you!"

"And I'm thankful, too," Grumpy Bear chimed in.

"You are?" asked Cheer.

"Well, I *wasn't* thankful for anything until my friends came along," Grumpy said.

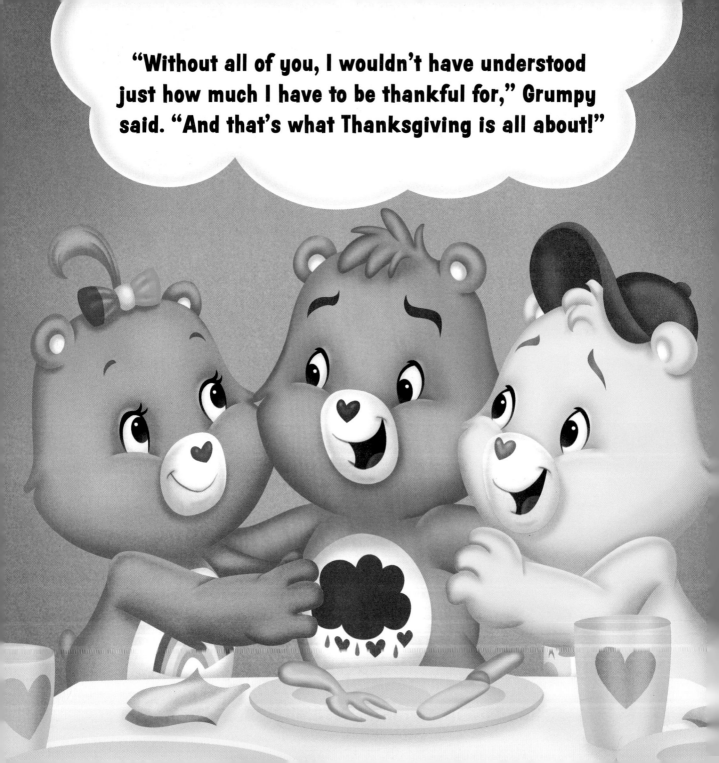